From Fish
to Fossil

Acknowledgments
Executive Editor: Diane Sharpe
Supervising Editor: Stephanie Muller
Design Manager: Sharon Golden
Page Design: Simon Balley Design Associates
Photography: Bruce Coleman: cover (bottom center, left, right),
pages 7 (all), 9, 19, 21, 23; Natural History Museum: cover (middle),
pages 24-25, 29; Topham Picture Source: page 16.

ISBN 0-8114-3791-4

From Fish
to Fossil

Mike Herschell

Illustrated by
Lynda Stevens

STECK-VAUGHN
COMPANY
ELEMENTARY • SECONDARY • ADULT • LIBRARY

A fossil is what remains of an animal
or plant that lived on Earth millions of
years ago.

People who study fossils are called
paleontologists. The study of fossils tells
us many things about life on Earth millions
of years ago.

It is the fossil of a fish that lived about 50 million years ago. The fossil has become a stone.

Millions of years ago, your fossil was once a fish living in a lake.

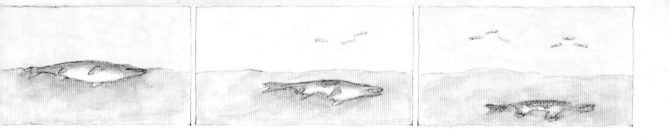

When the fish died, it sank to the bottom of the lake. Then it was covered by layers of sand and mud.

What did the sand and mud do?

The layers of sand and mud kept the bones of the fish together. After many years, the fish was buried deep under the lake.

After thousands of years, more and more
sand and mud pressed down on the fish.
It was pressed into the rock for so long
that it finally became part of the rock.

The fish turned
into rock!

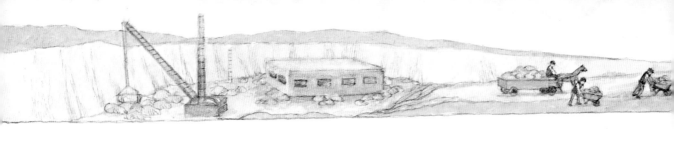

During the millions of years that passed, the lake slowly dried up. People needed rock for building houses, so they dug up the area with your fish fossil in it.

Will you show us some of the other fossils in the museum?

The museum has many fossils for us to see.
This one is called a trilobite.

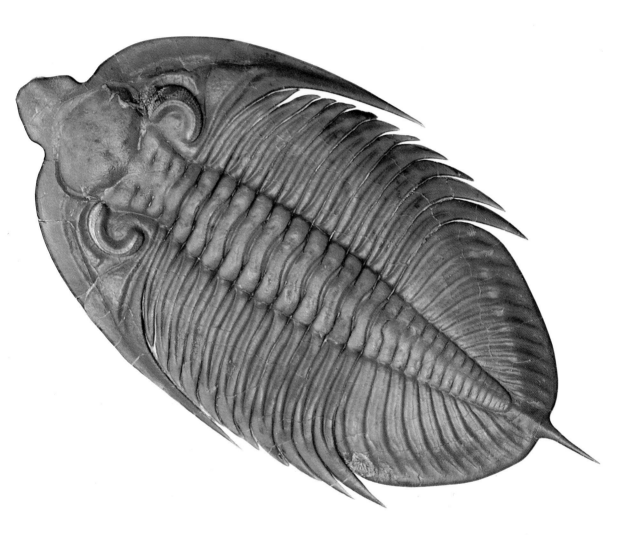

Trilobites lived in the ocean about
400 million years ago.

What's that beautiful fossil?

That is the fossil of a fern leaf from 300 million years ago. It became a fossil in the same way the fish did.

The leaf fell into mud. After millions of years, the mud turned to rock, and the leaf left a print of its shape.

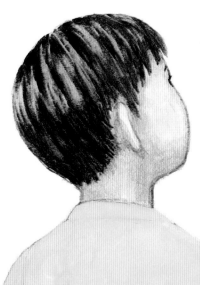

Is this fly a kind of fossil, too?

This is a very interesting fossil because the body of the fly did not rot like most fossils do.

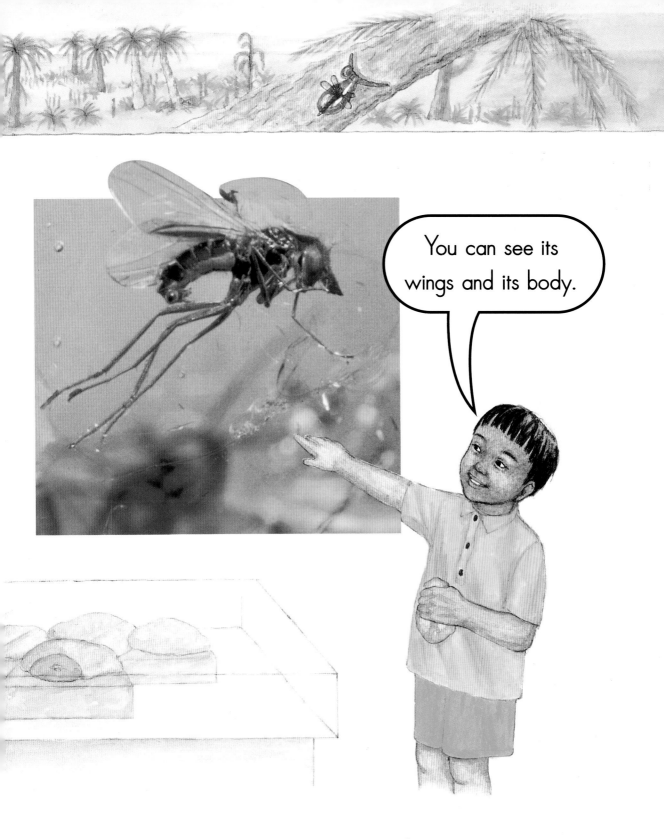

You can see its wings and its body.

The fly was trapped in a tree long ago.

That is the fossil of a Diplodocus skeleton.
This kind of dinosaur was one of the largest
creatures that ever lived. It may have
weighed as much as nine buses.

26

The Tyrannosaurus Rex was one of the largest meat-eating dinosaurs ever to roam Earth.

Did you know that its teeth were as long as knives?

Not all fossils are from plant and animal remains. This skull model is of a person who lived more than one million years ago.

Fossils tell us many interesting things about
life on Earth millions of years ago.

I'm going to look for more
fossils in the garden.

Look at the pictures. Can you remember how the fish became a fossil? The answers are on the last page, but don't look until you have tried naming each stage.

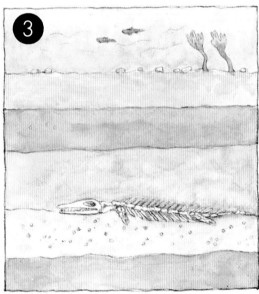

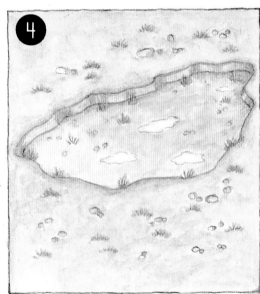

5

Index

Answers: 1. The fish dies and sinks to the bottom of the lake.
2. The fish is covered with sand and mud. 3. The fish turns into rock.
4. The lake dries up. 5. The rock with the fish fossil is dug up again.